First published in Belgium and Holland by Clavis Uitgeverij, Hasselt – Amsterdam, 2014
Copyright © 2014, Clavis Uitgeverij

English translation from the Dutch by Clavis Publishing Inc. New York
Copyright © 2015 for the English language edition: Clavis Publishing Inc. New York

Visit us on the web at www.clavisbooks.com

Little Dog Lost written and illustrated by Guido van Genechten
Original title: *Hondje*
Translated from the Dutch by Clavis Publishing

ISBN 978-1-60537-229-7

This book was printed in July 2015 at Proost Industries NV, Everdongenlaan 23, 2300 Turnhout, Belgium

First Edition
10 9 8 7 6 5 4 3 2 1

Clavis Publishing supports the First Amendment and celebrates the right to read

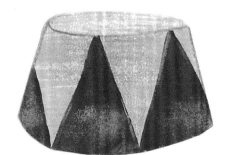

⚬~ Little Dog Lost ~⚬

GUIDO VAN GENECHTEN

Clavis

NEW YORK

Little Dog is Lost

He

searches

and

sniffs

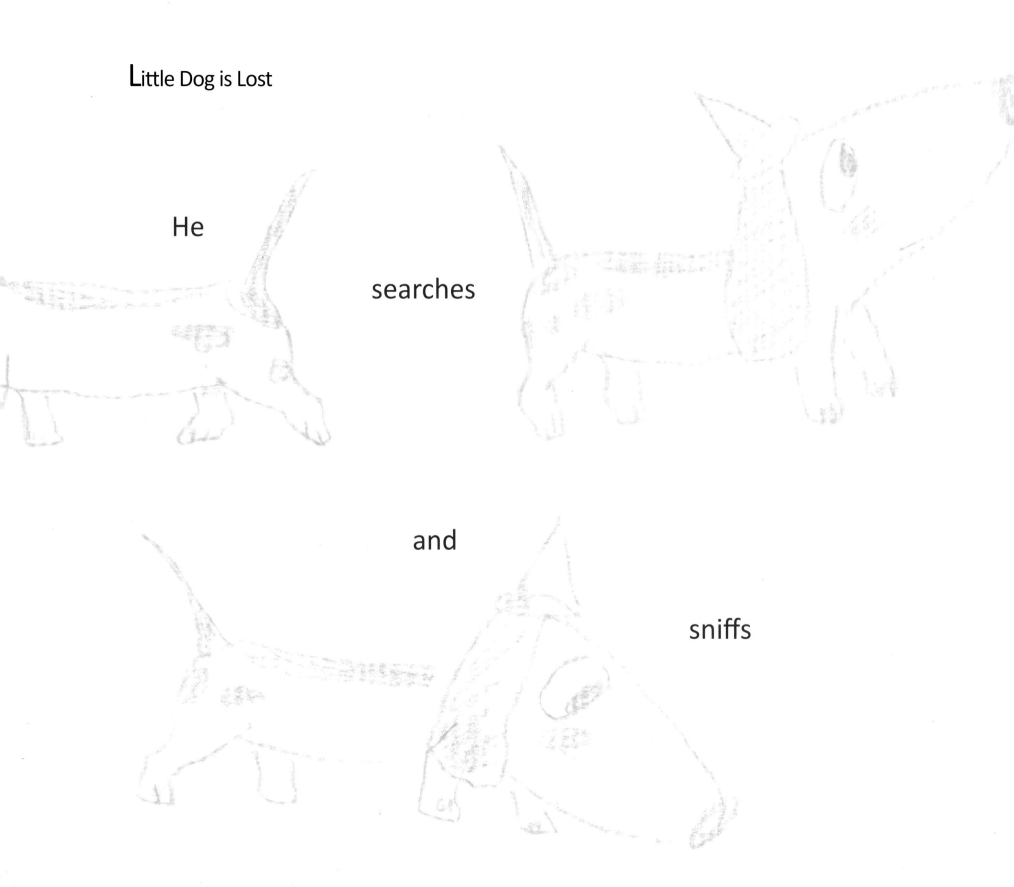

everywhere

Where did my owner go? Little Dog sighs.

No, this is not my owner. Little Dog shakes his ears.
My owner wears black shoes.
And he smells good. He doesn't have stinky toes.

Big black shoes with laces, a bit like these.
But about ten times as big,
because my owner has super long toes.

This morning he was wearing red socks.

My owner always wears red socks.

Red socks with white dots.

Or was it the other way around? Hmm….

A pair of bright yellow trousers! Found him! Uh oh no, my owner's trousers are checked....
Sorry, sir, I thought you were someone else. I'm looking for my loyal friend, my dear owner.

My owner smells delicious, like sawdust and sun-ripened pears. But my nose is confused by all these different smells.

My owner always carries a little umbrella, even when it's not raining. He says he can't do without it. Neither can I. Without my owner, I mean. Where did he go?

There's a plastic flower in the buttonhole of his jacket.

It's a white daisy that can cry. (It doesn't really cry, of course!

It is a complicated trick with tubes and things, and my owner told me not to tell anyone. Oops!)

I see flowers everywhere, but I don't see my owner.

My owner has the most beautiful nose in the world.
It's bright red and round and shiny,
like a ripe tomato in the sun.
But no matter how hard I look,
I can't find his nose anywhere.

What did you say?

Where?

Owner!

"Where were you, my sweet boy?
I looked everywhere for you."

"Come quickly, it's almost our turn."

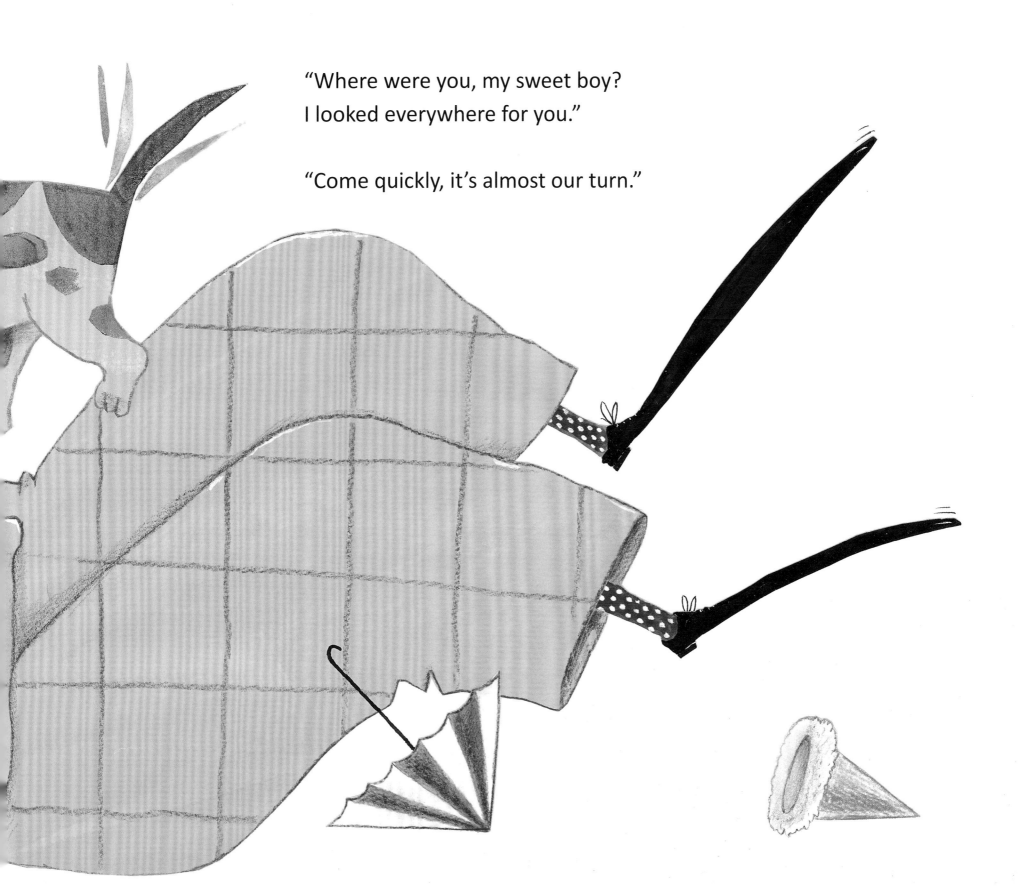

We want more!